PUFFIN BOOKS

Dancing Shoes

BEST FOOT FORWARD

Antonia Barber was born in London and grew up in Sussex. While studying English at London University, she spent her evenings at the Royal Opera House, where her father worked, watching the ballet and meeting many famous dancers. She married a fellow student and lived in New York before settling down in England. She has three children, including a daughter who did ballet from the age of three and attended the Royal Ballet School Junior Classes at Sadler's Wells.

Her best-known books are *The Ghosts*, which was runner-up for the Carnegie Medal and was filmed as *The Amazing Mr Blunden*, and *The Mousehole Cat*. She has also written *Tales from the Ballet*.

Antonia lives in an old oast house in Kent and a little fisherman's cottage in Cornwall.

If you like dancing and making friends, you'll love

DANCING SHOES

Lucy Lambert – Lou to her friends – dreams of one day becoming a great ballerina. Find out if Lucy's dream comes true in:

DANCING SHOES: LESSONS FOR LUCY
DANCING SHOES: INTO THE SPOTLIGHT
DANCING SHOES: FRIENDS AND RIVALS
DANCING SHOES: OUT OF STEP
DANCING SHOES: MAKING THE GRADE
DANCING SHOES: LUCY'S NEXT STEP

And look out for more DANCING SHOES titles
coming soon

Antonia Barber

DANCING SHOES
Best Foot Forward

Illustrated by Biz Hull

PUFFIN BOOKS

PUFFIN BOOKS

Published by the Penguin Group
Penguin Books Ltd, 27 Wrights Lane, London W8 5TZ, England
Penguin Putnam Inc., 375 Hudson Street, New York, New York 10014, USA
Penguin Books Australia Ltd, Ringwood, Victoria, Australia
Penguin Books Canada Ltd, 10 Alcorn Avenue, Toronto, Ontario, Canada M4V 3B2
Penguin Books (NZ) Ltd, Private Bag 102902, NSMC, Auckland, New Zealand

On the World Wide Web at: www.penguin.com

Penguin Books Ltd, Registered Offices: Harmondsworth, Middlesex, England

First published 1999
1 3 5 7 9 10 8 6 4 2

Text copyright © Antonia Barber, 1999
Illustrations copyright © Biz Hull, 1999
All rights reserved

Made and printed in England by Clays Ltd, St Ives plc

British Library Cataloguing in Publication Data
A CIP catalogue record for this book is available from the British Library

ISBN 0–141–30527–4

Chapter One

'Are you sure you'll bc all right, Emma?'

'I'll be fine. Really, I will!'

'Oh, I do wish I wasn't doing this course today!' Mrs Browne looked really guilty. 'Just when you are starting your new school . . .'

Emma sighed. 'It's OK,' she said. 'I'll be going with Lou . . . and her mum . . . and Charlie.'

'We'll look after her,' said Lou. She knew that Emma was secretly relieved that her mother wasn't taking her to school on the first day.

'The last thing I need,' she had confided to Lou, 'is to arrive in a posh car and have my mum fussing over me in front of everyone.'

Mrs Browne looked at her watch. 'I ought to be going,' she said. 'Now, are you sure, Emma?'

They practically had to push her out of the door.

Standing on the front steps, waving as the big estate car pulled away, the two girls breathed a sigh of relief.

'Mothers are such a worry,' said Emma.

'Aren't they just!' agreed Lou.

The car disappeared around the corner and the girls rushed inside, slamming the front door behind them. They raced down the basement stairs to Lou's flat, where

Jenny Lambert, Lou's mother, was just
wiping the last traces of breakfast from
Charlie's face.

'Hi, Charlie,' said Emma. 'Who's going
to a new school today?'

'Teddy!' said Charlie, waving his
beloved bear at her.

'*And* Charlie?' said Emma.

'Teddy *and* Charlie,' he agreed.

'Teddy and Charlie *and* Emma,' Lou told him. 'You're going to playgroup and Emma is coming to school with me.'

'And Emma's mum has gone to hairdressing school,' said Jenny, 'so it's a big day all round. And what's more,' she added, glancing up at the clock, 'if we don't put our best foot forward, we're all going to be late!'

Everyone panicked for five minutes and then suddenly they were ready. Lou and Emma bumped Charlie's pushchair up the basement steps.

The morning was clear and bright after days of rain. Leaves were beginning to drift from the trees along the street.

Summer was ending, thought Lou, as they waited for the traffic lights to change. Everyone seemed to be starting something new. Emma's mother was going back to

4

work: she was doing a course to learn about new hairstyles. Emma's dad, who had once had an important job in a bank, was starting again as a carpenter. Even her own mother was looking for a part-time job to do once Charlie had settled into playgroup. And Emma had left her private girls' school, where she had never been very happy, to join Lou at the local primary.

The lights changed and they crossed the road.

'It will be strange going to school with boys,' said Emma suddenly. She sounded rather nervous.

'You get on very well with Jem,' said Lou's mother.

'Yes, but Jem's different,' said Emma. 'I mean, he goes to ballet . . .'

Lou hooted. 'Don't let him hear you say

that!' she warned. 'He's always trying to prove that he's *not* different, just because he does ballet.'

'Well, no,' said Emma, 'but you know what I mean. Most boys are much . . . rougher.'

Lou could see that Emma was in for a

few shocks. The truth was that at school
Jem was often the ringleader when the
boys were into some mischief. He was
Lou and Emma's special friend, the only
boy in their ballet class. At the Maple
School of Ballet, dance was a strong bond
that brought the three friends together, but
at day school it was another matter. Jem
was a year older, so they weren't even in
the same class. And at break-time boys
hung about together and rarely talked to
the girls.

'I don't suppose we'll see much of him,'
Lou told Emma, 'except perhaps on the
way home.'

Emma looked disappointed.

They had left the tree-lined streets
behind and were passing a big estate with
rows of small houses and blocks of tall
flats. Lou looked out for Melanie and

Tracey, who lived near by. They were her school friends, but because she lived some way away she didn't see them very often out of school. Tracey and Melanie lived close to one another and were each other's best friends. Lou's best friend was Emma, and they were even closer because they lived in the same house. Lou wondered uneasily whether Tracey and Melanie would take to Emma. If they don't, she thought, I may have problems . . .

Chapter Two

'Melanie can walk on her hands,' said Tracey.

It was lunch-time and they were in the playground.

Melanie tucked her skirt up into her knickers and showed off her skill. The beads jingled in her braided hair.

'Can you do that?' Tracey asked Emma.

Emma shook her head. 'No,' she said, 'I always fall over.'

'She's teaching me,' said Tracey proudly.

Melanie turned right way up again and said, 'I've been teaching you all summer, Trace, and you still can't do it.'

'No,' said Tracey humbly, 'but I am trying.'

'*Very* trying,' said Melanie drily.

Tracey laughed at the joke.

Watching them, Lou thought, as she often did, that they were an odd pair. Melanie was tall and slim, good at gymnastics and clever in class. Tracey was short, solid and not very good at anything. With nothing to boast about herself, she boasted about her best friend instead. 'Melanie can do cartwheels too,' she told Emma.

Melanie did one.

'So can Emma,' said Lou, who felt that Melanie was getting altogether too much attention, 'and so can I.'

They both proved it.

'You're not as good as Melanie, though,' said Tracey.

Lou thought this was probably true. 'Well, Melanie does gym,' she pointed out, 'and we do ballet.'

'Melanie can stand on one leg,' said Tracey, 'like ballet dancers do!'

It turned into a balancing-on-one-leg competition . . . which Melanie won.

'Actually, we haven't done arabesques yet,' Emma explained.

'Oh, *ectually* we haven't done *erobics* yet,' said Tracey, mocking her.

Emma looked really embarrassed.

'*Arabesques* not *aerobics*,' said Lou. 'Get your ears washed, Tracey.'

Melanie laughed, so Tracey laughed too, and the awkward moment passed. But Lou thought she could see trouble ahead. She wondered if Tracey was afraid that Melanie might like the new girl better than her, that she might want Emma for her best friend instead. Well, she needn't worry, thought Lou, because Emma is *my* best friend and no one is going to change that.

But she did so want Emma to become part of the group. After all, it was because she had been bullied and left out at her other school that Emma had come to school with Lou.

'Let's walk round the field,' she said, hoping a change of scene might mean a change of subject.

As they reached the playing field, they passed a group of boys coming back from football practice. They were covered in mud from the rain-soaked pitch and one of them called out, 'Hi, Emma, how's it going?' as he went by.

At once the others took up the cry: 'Hi, Emma!', 'Hello, Emma!', 'Oh, Emma, Emma!', 'How are you today, Emma?'

Emma put her head down and flushed bright pink.

Lou shouted, 'Mudlarks!' It was what Grandad called her when they went digging for worms on the beach in Cornwall.

Melanie and Tracey shouted something
rather ruder.

'However did they know my name?'
asked Emma, looking desperately at Lou.

'Well,' said Lou, trying hard not to
laugh. 'The first one was Jem.'

'*Really!*' Emma was astonished. She
turned and stared after them.

One of the muddy figures waved and

pranced about. The others followed suit.

'They're just being friendly,' said Lou, grinning.

Emma's face went back to its usual colour.

'Loosen up, Em,' said Lou. 'You're going to have to get used to having boys around.'

'They're a pretty stupid lot,' said Tracey scornfully. 'You just have to give as good as you get.' Now it was boys against girls, so she was on Emma's side.

At the end of the day, when they had parted from the other girls and were walking home together, Emma said, 'I don't say "ectually", Lou, do I?'

Lou could see that she was still smarting. 'Of course you don't!' she said. 'Tracey was just getting at you because you talk a bit posher than she does.'

'I don't talk any posher than you do,' said Emma indignantly.

'I know you don't. It's just because she knows you went to a private school.'

They walked in silence for a while and then Lou said, 'Tracey's a bit funny sometimes, Em. She's . . . well, she's got her own problems . . . but she's all right really. You'll get used to each other after a bit.'

'I suppose so,' said Emma, but she didn't seem too sure.

A bike pulled up beside them and Jem said, 'How did the first day go, Em?'

She brightened. 'Oh, not too bad,' she said.

'*You* didn't help by setting your football team on to her,' Lou told him crossly.

'Didn't she like them?' Jem was

surprised. He turned to Emma. 'They liked you,' he told her.

Emma blushed. 'Did they?' she said.

Lou thought she sounded pleased.

'Oh yes!' said Jem. 'They thought you were very upmarket!'

Emma didn't understand.

'You know . . . sort of . . . *posh*,' he explained.

Lou groaned.

Chapter Three

It was good to be back in the changing room of the Maple School of Ballet.

There were a few nervous newcomers among the younger children. They watched, wide-eyed, as the others crowded around Lou and Emma, greeting them like old friends.

But at the far end of the room things had changed. Where once Angela had queened it over everyone, there were now two distinct groups. Some still stood around the tall, blonde girl, but others clustered around Paula, who had been Angela's best friend until they had quarrelled at the Summer School.

Paula's group came across to Emma.

'Hi!' said Paula, smiling brightly. 'What's your new school like?'

'Oh . . .' Emma seemed surprised. 'It's great,' she said.

'We *were* sorry to hear about your father,' said another girl. 'Losing his job, I mean.'

Emma was just peeling off her sweat-shirt. As her face emerged, Lou saw that she was frowning. Lou stepped in quickly.

'Emma's dad didn't *lose* his job,' she said. 'He gave it up because he didn't want to do banking any more.'

'Oh, *really*!' The girl sounded as if she

didn't believe a word. 'So, what does he do now?' she asked.

'He's a carpenter,' said Emma.

'A *carpenter*? Really!' said Paula. 'I suppose that's why he can't afford your school fees . . .'

'Who says he can't?' Emma was getting really cross.

'Well, Sophie told me, actually . . . I think she heard it from Angela.'

'Well, it's *not true*!' Emma raised her voice. 'If you must know, I'm going to Lou and Jem's school because I've always wanted to go there, just like my dad has always wanted to be a carpenter!' She clenched her fists as she glanced across at Angela, but the blonde girl was just disappearing through the changing-room door.

Paula shrugged her shoulders. 'No need

to get steamed up about it,' she said
huffily.

Her group moved away, muttering
among themselves, leaving Lou and
Emma alone.

'Don't let them get to you, Em,' said
Lou comfortingly. 'Here, I'd better do your
hair.'

'I thought Angela would leave me alone once I'd left that school,' said Emma miserably.

'Well, I expect it's because you stood up to her,' said Lou. 'She won't forgive you for that. But you mustn't let her upset you, because that's what she wants. If she thinks you don't care, then you'll be the winner.'

Emma tried to put on a smile.

'Quick, fix my hair,' said Lou, trying to distract her, 'or we'll be late for class.'

In the ballet studio, Angela was talking to Jem. He left her and came across. 'What's up, Em?' he asked, seeing her unhappy face. But Emma shook her head and walked on.

'I'll tell you about it later,' hissed Lou. 'Just cheer her up . . . make her feel important.'

Jem grinned. 'Got it!' he said and went after Emma.

As they waited, he stood joking with her while the other girls looked on enviously. Lou watched them. Jem was very useful, she thought. As the only boy in the class, all the girls wanted to be friends with him . . . especially the ones from the girls' school, who didn't seem to know many boys. Emma was beginning to smile. It was hard to keep a straight face when Jem was trying to make you laugh.

Mrs Dennison came in and the class began. Most of the girls were out of practice after the long summer break, but Lou, Emma and Jem had kept up their practice classes with old Mrs Dillon, who lived on the top floor of the Brownes' house. As a young woman she had danced with the Russian Bolshoi company, and she had given Lou her first ballet lessons.

'Next *battements tendus*,' called Mrs
Dennison.

Lou thought about the postcard that had
come from Shell that morning. They had
made friends with Shell Pink at the
Summer School. (*First position . . . hand on
waist . . . head up*.) The postcard had a
ballerina in a white tutu on the front and
it was all about a dance festival where
Shell had just performed. (*Three* tendus *to
second . . . and close into first . . .*) She was
always doing festivals and winning prizes.

'Lucy, please keep your mind on your
dancing.' Mrs Dennison's voice was sharp.

Lou tried to concentrate. She saw Jem
was grinning, but not for long.

'You too, Jem!' said Mrs Dennison. 'I
don't know what's wrong with you all
today.'

Shell is always winning prizcs, thought
Lou, and I haven't won any . . . well, only
one . . . and I haven't done any festivals.
She wondered if it would count against
her when she wanted to get into ballet
school. (. . . *and down into* demi-plié . . .
and stretch . . .) She couldn't really ask
Mrs Dennison about it – she would just
say, 'You certainly won't get in, Lucy, if
you don't concentrate on your work!'
She decided to ask Miss Ashton instead.

They hung about on the front steps
waiting for Miss Ashton to come out.
They all liked her. She had taught Lou
and Emma in the Beginners' Class and
they had done a pantomime together.
Then she had taught all three of them at
the Summer School.

'Do you think we'll be in the

pantomime this year?' asked Emma hopefully.

'I doubt it,' said Lou gloomily, 'not if we did it last year.'

'But we were Beginners then. It might be our class's turn this year.'

'If it is, they'll probably choose Angela and Paula and that lot,' said Lou.

'And me,' said Jem cheerfully. '*I* didn't do it last year.'

The two girls frowned. They didn't like that idea at all. Doing a show brought people close together and they didn't want Jem being friends with Angela and Paula instead of them . . .

Miss Ashton came out and they walked along with her.

'When we try to get into ballet school,' Lou asked, 'will it matter if we haven't won lots of prizes . . . like Shell, I mean?'

Miss Ashton smiled and shook her
head. 'Not a bit,' she said. 'They will be
interested in the standards you have
reached but not how many exams you
have taken or how many cups you have
won. The thing that will matter most is
whether you are the right size and shape.
Ballet puts a great strain on your body, so

you must have the right build and flexibility. You need a good sense of music and rhythm too . . . and you have to be able to learn steps quickly and remember them.'

They went on without talking while Lou tried to decide whether she had any chance. Seeing her worried face, Miss Ashton said, 'I think you should do quite well, Lucy.'

'Do you?' Lou looked up hopefully.

'And did you know,' said Miss Ashton, 'that if you do get in, they will teach you all over again, right from the beginning?'

They looked horrified and she laughed.

'What . . . first position and *pliés* and all that?' demanded Lou.

'Yes, all that!'

They had reached the corner where their ways parted. As they said goodbye,

Jem said, 'I don't suppose there's any news yet about the pantomime?'

'Ah . . .' Miss Ashton looked cautious. 'I'm not supposed to tell you before Miss Maple makes the announcement,' she said, 'but . . . well, don't get your hopes up.'

They watched miserably as she went away down the road.

'That means we're not in it,' said Lou.

The day suddenly seemed very dull . . . almost like winter.

Chapter Four

It was Saturday morning and they met up in the street market. Lou thought that if they spent more time with Tracey and Melanie out of school, the two girls would get to know Emma better. It was really awkward, she thought, when you had two sets of friends and they didn't really get on together. Emma tried hard to be friendly and Melanie was quite easygoing, as long as you admired her skill at gym. The problem was Tracey. She had got it into

her head that Emma thought she was
something special and so she was always
trying to bring the new girl down.

Lou had imagined a sunny autumn
morning spent sorting through the stalls of
bright scarves and hair-ties, cheap
jewellery, old comics, sweets and other
odds and ends. Unfortunately, there was a
drizzling rain that put a real damper on
the whole outing.

Then the Wind-up Merchant appeared.
He was Angela's grandfather but he was
also Lou and Emma's friend ever since
they had done the pantomime together.
Lou looked around for Angela, but she
was nowhere to be seen.

'What miserable weather,' said the
Wind-up Merchant. 'Does anyone fancy a
hot drink and a cream cake?'

'We've got our friends with us,' Lou

explained, nodding towards Melanie and Tracey, who looked up suspiciously.

'Bring them along,' said the Wind-up Merchant cheerfully.

Tracey glared at him. 'I'm not allowed to talk to strange men,' she said.

'Oh, but this is Mr Mumford,' said Lou. 'He's a friend of my mum.'

'And he's my dad's business partner,' added Emma.

The Wind-up Merchant laughed. 'I suppose I am a bit strange,' he said, 'and Tracey is quite right. Why don't I find your mum, Lou, and Charlie, then we can all go together?'

When he had gone in search of them, Tracey said accusingly, 'He's that Angela's grandfather, and he's really rich and snobby!'

'No, he's not!' said Lou indignantly.

'Well, I mean, he is rich, I suppose, but he's not snobby.'

'How can he be your dad's partner,' said Tracey to Emma, 'if your dad's only a carpenter?'

'Well, they make fitted kitchens. Mr Mumford runs the business and my dad makes all the cupboards and things.'

'You mean he works for the other bloke?' said Tracey.

'Sort of . . .' Emma thought it was best not to try to explain.

'Well, you should say that,' said Tracey, 'and not pretend he's a partner.'

'But he is . . .' began Lou.

Emma shook her head at her, so she gave up.

'Trying to make herself look important,' muttered Tracey so that they could just hear.

Lou and Emma pretended that they hadn't heard.

The Wind-up Merchant came back with Jenny Lambert and Charlie and soon they were all settled around a big table in the Cosy Corner teashop. Melanie and Tracey sat uneasily looking around them. The

Cosy Corner had the best cream cakes in town but it was rather expensive.

When she saw the prices, Tracey's face fell. She turned to Lou. 'Who's paying?' she hissed.

'It's all right,' whispered Lou. 'Mr Mumford invited us.'

'But I'm not allowed to take sweets and things from strange men,' said Tracey.

Lou groaned. 'I told you, he's my mum's friend,' she pointed out.

'Yes, but he's not *my* mum's friend,' said Traccy.

Lou could see that she was bent on being awkward. She got up, went round the table and spoke quietly to her mother, who nodded. Then Jenny looked up and smiled. 'Oh, didn't I explain?' she said brightly. 'It's my treat today because we're celebrating my new job.'

This caused great excitement.

'You got the job!' said Lou. 'Oh, great!'

She knew her mum had been waiting to hear.

'The letter came this morning,' said Jenny, 'just after you went out.'

Lou was thrilled. She hugged her mother and then hugged Charlie. At last, she thought, things were beginning to change! They had been hard up ever since her father had died, two years before. She only had ballet lessons because the Maple School had given her a free scholarship.

'Tell me about the job,' she said eagerly.

'Well, it's just right for me,' said her mother. 'I'm going to be a research assistant to one of the professors at the university. He's writing a book and he needs help with finding things out and word-processing.'

'All that stuff you did at evening class?' said Lou.

'All that stuff,' agreed Jenny. 'But the best thing is that I shall do the research at the college in the mornings, while Charlie is at playgroup. Then I can do the word-processing at home in the afternoons while he is having his sleep or after he's in bed.'

'But we haven't got a computer.'

'The professor is lending me one.'

'Oh, wow!' Lou's eyes lit up. 'Can we get some games?'

'Well, I don't know . . . I'll have to think about that.'

'What about the holidays?'

'Well, most of the work will be in term time.'

'Couldn't be better!' said Mr Mumford. 'I'm so pleased for you.'

'Melanie's mum works in the theatre,' said Tracey loudly. It was clear that she had heard enough about Lou's mum's job.

'Does she?' Emma was delighted. Like Lou, she loved anything to do with the theatre.

'At the hospital,' added Tracey.

'I didn't know they had a theatre at the hospital,' said Emma with interest. She imagined all the patients with their arms and legs in plaster, sitting in the audience watching a colourful musical. She felt sure

it would help them to get better faster.

'In the *operating* theatre,' said Melanie, giving Tracey a crushing look. 'She's a theatre nurse,' she explained.

Emma looked disappointed and Jenny said quickly, 'She must be very clever, Melanie.'

'Yes, she is,' said Melanie proudly.

'And her dad's on the railway,' added Tracey, 'so she gets to travel for free.'

'Sometimes,' said Melanie.

The waitress was hovering with her little order book.

'Well, now,' said the Wind-up Merchant. 'Have you all made up your minds what you want?'

They turned their attention back to the big shiny menu.

Nobody asked about Tracey's parents.

Chapter Five

It was nearly half-term. Lou couldn't believe how quickly the weeks had passed.

Emma was settling in well. Melanie was quite friendly now and Liza Tompkins told Lou that the other girls thought Emma was 'really nice'. She was also learning how to deal with the boys. Their digs no longer upset her and she could shout 'Get lost!' and 'In your dreams!' with the rest of the girls. Jem said he was proud of her.

'The boys still think she's a bit posh,' he

told Lou. 'They quite like it when she tells them off!'

Lou laughed. 'Don't tell her that,' she said. 'She already thinks they're weird enough.'

'How's she getting on with Tracey?'

Lou sighed. 'Well, Tracey still keeps getting at her. Em tries not to mind, but I know it hurts her.'

At that moment, Emma came running along the street to join them. They were on their way home from ballet class and she had left her shoes behind.

'They were under the bench,' she puffed. 'They must have got kicked out of sight.'

They walked on together.

'Shame about the pantomime,' said Jem.

Gloomily Lou and Emma agreed. It had been announced that the dramatic society was doing *Aladdin* this year and wanted older girls from the ballet school's senior classes to be harem dancers.

'I suppose it *is* best to have the older ones,' said Emma reasonably. 'I mean, if they have to wear veils and things.'

Lou had her own opinion about that. She had worn a harem outfit herself, when she had helped the Wind-up Merchant with the magic at Angela's party. She thought she had looked really neat in it and had dearly wanted the chance to repeat her success. Remembering that day, she said, 'We shan't get invited to Angela's party this year.'

'I don't know who will be,' said Emma. 'I mean, she seems to have quarrelled with most of her friends.'

'I expect she'll invite me,' said Jem, grinning.

'Well, lucky old you,' said Lou huffily. 'You can have her all to yourself!'

Jem fooled about. He cringed and pulled his jacket up over his head as if trying to hide from her.

The girls ignored him.

'Her birthday's not for ages, anyway,' said Emma. 'But mine is quite soon, Lou, so you can come to my party instead.'

'Are you having a party?' Lou was surprised.

Last year, when Emma didn't have many friends, she had chosen a birthday outing to the ballet instead. They had gone to the Opera House and sat in a box. Lou had rather hoped they would go again this year.

'Well . . . it's for my mum really,' explained Emma. 'She loves giving parties for me and I wouldn't let her last year. But

now that I've got lots of new friends . . .'

'Yes, of course,' said Lou, quickly
hiding her disappointment. 'It'll be great,
Emma! Who are you going to invite?'

Jem emerged from his coat and pranced
around Emma with his 'hopeful' face on
until she laughed and said, 'Oh, all right,
you can come.'

Lou did the same.

'Well, of course *you* are coming, Lou,' said Emma. 'Stop mucking about, you two!' Then her face went all serious. 'But there is a snag!' she told them.

'Tracey?' said Lou.

'Worse!' said Emma. 'My mum says, because I went to her party last year, I'll have to invite Angela.'

Lou made a face.

'Oh, just sit her next to Tracey,' said Jem, 'then they can both be horrible to each other.'

'The mind boggles!' said Lou.

At school next day there was good news. Mrs Merridew, the head teacher, made an announcement about the end-of-term concert. Anyone who wanted to take part had to see Miss Johnson in the gym at lunch break.

Lou, Emma and Jem were among the
first to arrive and it turned out to be really
exciting. Usually the Christmas concert
was a mixture of poems and carols and
things. But Miss Johnson was a new
teacher and she wanted to do a real
musical.

The story was about an old fisherman
and his cat who went out in a great storm.
The people in the village were very hungry
because the sea was too rough to go
fishing. When Christmas came, the old
fisherman could not bear to see the
children starving, so he braved the storm
and saved them all.

'The story,' said Miss Johnson, 'is called
The Mousehole Cat.'

At once Lou's hand was in the air,
waving wildly.

'Yes?' said Miss Johnson.

'Please, miss!' Lou was bursting with
excitement. 'That's where my grandad and
grandma live . . . in Mousehole, miss . . .
in Cornwall!'

This caused a great stir and Lou became
the centre of attention.

'Really?' Miss Johnson was very interested. She asked if Lou had any photographs or postcards of the village which might help with the scenery. Lou said she had lots and promised to bring them in.

I'll phone Grandad and tell him, she thought. He would be thrilled. She was so busy thinking what she would say to him that she forgot to listen to what Miss Johnson was saying until she had almost finished.

'. . . and some to play the children and, lastly, a lot of cats.'

Hands shot up. 'Me, miss! Can I be a cat, miss?' There was a lot of 'miaowing' as they all showed how well they would do it.

Miss Johnson hushed them. 'For today,' she said, 'I just need a list of names and what you like doing best: singing, acting, dancing, playing music, painting scenery, making costumes.'

'This is going to be even better than doing the pantomime,' said Jem as they went back to their classes. 'I mean, this time we'll be doing *everything*.'

Chapter Six

Mrs Browne had gone right Over The Top.

'I tried to keep it fairly simple,' Emma told Lou when they were alone, 'but Mum just loves doing parties and when she'd bought all the stuff . . . and she was *so* excited about it . . . well, I didn't like to spoil her fun.'

'But it's *your* birthday party,' Lou pointed out. 'I mean, it's supposed to be fun for *you*, not your mum.' There were times, she thought, when Emma seemed

more like the mother and Mrs Browne like
the daughter. 'Why don't you just tell her?'
she said. 'I mean, it's like Balloon City in
here!'

'I *can't*! I can't bear it when she looks
disappointed . . .'

Lou smiled at Emma's anxious face.
'Oh, honestly!' she said, giving her friend
a sudden hug. 'You're just too nice for
your own good!'

All the balloons and decorations didn't exactly help when Melanie and Tracey arrived early.

'Wow!' said Melanie. 'Does your dad own a balloon factory?'

'They only put up a few,' said Lou quickly, 'but we think they've been breeding in the night.'

Melanie thought this was really funny, so Tracey stopped glaring at the balloons and laughed too. But she seemed put out by the size of the house.

'Do your mum and dad own this house?' she demanded.

'Er . . . yes,' said Emma.

'Melanie's mum and dad own their house too!' said Tracey triumphantly. 'They bought it off the council!'

'It's not as big as this one though,' said

Melanie, looking round admiringly at the spacious room.

Tracey frowned. 'Do you live in all the house?' she asked Emma.

'No,' said Emma quickly. She felt that maybe Tracey wouldn't mind the house being so big if she knew it was shared. 'Lou and her mum and Charlie live downstairs and Mrs Dillon on the top floor.'

'Well then, you don't own *all* the house, do you?' said Tracey. 'Melanie owns *all* her house.'

She made it sound as if Emma was telling lies, which made Lou cross. 'Actually, they do own all of the house,' she told Tracey. 'We just rent part of it.' Too late, she saw her mistake.

'*You* pay *rent*,' said Tracey disapprovingly, 'to Emma's dad?'

'Well . . . yes,' said Lou.

'So your dad is a *landlord* then,' said
Tracey, turning to Emma. 'My mum says
landlords live off the poor and they
shouldn't be allowed!'

Emma looked really upset and Lou was
furious.

'Some landlords are awful,' she said. 'I
know, because we had one before Mr
Browne bought the house. But Emma's
dad is great! He fixed new kitchens for us
and made window-boxes and things. So if
you say anything bad about him, Tracey
Gibbs, you'll have me to deal with!'

Tracey stuck out her lip and looked
ready for a fight, but Melanie said wearily,
'Shut up, Trace! You're spoiling the party,'
and Tracey collapsed like a pricked
balloon.

Luckily, Jem arrived at that moment
with a group of other boys. Emma had

wanted Jem at her party but he didn't fancy being the only boy, so Mrs Browne had told him cheerfully to 'bring along all his friends'. He had taken her at her word and for a while the boys outnumbered the girls. Quite a few of the balloons got popped one way and another, which wasn't a bad thing. Then lots of other girls arrived, including Angela with two of her friends. Mrs Browne had been very generous with the invitations, anxious that they should all enjoy themselves. Soon the house was crowded and everyone, even Tracey and Angela, seemed to be having a good time.

When it was all over, Lou and Emma were left amid the ruins. They lay on a heap of cushions, feebly blowing party squeakers.

'We'll be living on sausage rolls and birthday cake for a week,' said Emma.

'Suits me!' said Lou. 'Your mum did a smashing tea!'

'Do you think they enjoyed it?' said Emma.

'It was great!' said Lou. 'Even Angela looked quite human at times.'

'Tracey seemed to be getting on well with all the boys.' Emma sounded surprised. 'Usually she hasn't got a good word for them.'

Lou laughed. 'I spoke to Jem,' she said. 'Told him it was "Keep Tracey Happy Day".'

They flopped in silence for a while. Then Emma sat up suddenly. 'I'd almost forgotten,' she said. 'I've got another present to come.'

'Haven't you had enough?' said Lou without envy.

'This one's different,' said Emma. 'Mum says it's something I've always wanted, but I had to wait till the party was over.'

'Must be something that breaks easily.'

'Yes, I think so. I know she took it up to Mrs Dillon's flat for safety.'

They went to look for Mrs Browne and

met her coming down the stairs. In her arms was a box and in the box was a small basket . . . and in the basket there were two kittens.

Chapter Seven

Emma had been pleading for a pet for a long time and the Brownes had said that they would think about getting a cat.

'But *two kittens*!' said Emma. 'Oh, they are so *sweet*!'

'We found them at the Cat Rescue Home,' said Mrs Browne. 'They are sisters and they were having such fun together, we felt we couldn't part them.'

'Oh, you are so lucky, Em,' sighed Lou. 'I wish we could have a kitten.'

'Well,' said Mrs Browne, 'that was the idea, that you should have one each.'

Lou could hardly believe her luck. It wasn't even her birthday! 'But what will Mum say?' she asked.

'I've spoken to Jenny and she says it will be fine . . . only we think they should both stay up here until they are a bit bigger.'

'Because they would be lonely if we separated them?' said Emma.

Lou laughed. 'Because they wouldn't be safe downstairs with Charlie around,' she said.

'Well . . . a bit of both,' said Mrs
Browne tactfully.

Charlie was getting very rough since he
had started at playgroup. He had met a lot
of other little boys there and his new
friends jumped on each other and wrestled
a lot. They also shouted, threw things
about and laughed very loudly.

'It's like watching *Toddlers Behaving
Badly*,' Lou had complained to her mother.

But Jenny didn't seem too worried.
'He's just going through a stage,' she said.
'You were a Terrible Toddler once and you
grew out of it.'

It did seem best for the kittens to live
with Emma for a while, but Lou couldn't
bear to be parted from them, so she
fetched her quilt upstairs to Emma's room
that night.

'What are we going to call them?' asked

Emma as they lay on the floor, trailing paper butterflies for the kittens to chase.

'Oh, Valentina and Anastasia,' said Lou.

'Oh, yes, of course!' Emma was delighted. Anastasia and Valentina were the two ballerinas whose adventures the girls made up whenever they slept in Emma's room together.

They watched until the kittens grew tired and fell asleep, curled together in the little basket. Five minutes later Lou and Emma were asleep too.

The notice went up at school next day. Lou got there first.

'Oh, fantastic!' She turned to Emma and Jem, who were close behind. 'We are going to be the *Cats*!' she told them.

Jem studied the list more closely. 'It's the dancers,' he said. 'All those who said they wanted to dance are Cats . . . Oh, and some like Mel who are good at gym.'

'We must be doing a Cat dance or something,' said Emma eagerly. 'Oh, Lou! Won't it be great? Like being Rats in the pantomime.' Emma loved performing in an animal mask. It wasn't quite so scary if the audience couldn't see your face.

Melanie arrived.

'We're playing the Cats,' Lou told her.

'Oh, great!' said Tracey, coming up bchind.

'Well . . . not you, Trace,' said Lou. 'You're going to be –' She looked quickly at the list. 'You're one of the Village Children.' She tried to make it sound exciting.

Tracey's face fell. '*Boring*!' she said. 'I want to be a Cat, like Mel.'

'Well, the Cats all seem to be people who do dance . . . or gym,' Lou explained.

Tracey scowled. 'Just because my mum can't afford lessons, I get left out. I bet *she* gets to be a Cat!' she said, glaring at Emma.

'Yes, well, she does ballet,' said Melanie. 'Stop making a fuss about nothing, Trace!'

Tracey went quiet but Lou could see that she was angry. She wondered if this would make her even worse towards Emma.

They had a rehearsal at lunch-time and there was a surprise in store for them. Miss Johnson came into the hall, followed by an old friend.

'We are very lucky,' she told them, 'to have Miss Ashton, who teaches at the Maple School of Ballet. She has come

today to help you work out the steps for
your Cat dances.'

The class was great fun. To begin with,
Miss Ashton asked them all to think about
a cat they knew. Lou and Emma thought
about the kittens.

'I want you to imagine that you are
that cat. You could be walking, running,
jumping, waking up, stretching, curling up
to sleep or drinking a saucer of milk. But
whatever you do, you must try to move
just the way the cat would move.'

'Remember how we used to do this in
the Beginners' Class,' said Lou to Emma,
'being cats and rabbits and things?'

They stretched and prowled and tried to
be as cat-like as they could. Emma thought
of the way Valentina put up her tiny paws
to catch the paper butterflies. She lifted her
hands and gently pawed the air.

'That's very good, Emma.' It was Miss Ashton's voice and Emma went quite pink with pleasure.

And then, just at that moment, she looked up and caught sight of Tracey. She was standing outside in the corridor, peering in through one of the little windows in the hall door. But she didn't look mean or sulky now . . . she just looked really miserable . . . and very much alone.

Chapter Eight

'We've got to do something about Tracey,'
said Emma to Lou and Jem as they
walked home from school.

'She's a pain, isn't she?' said Lou. 'I'm
sorry she's giving you a bad time, Em.'

'No, you don't understand,' said Emma.
'We've got to get her into the Cat dance.'

'The Cat dance!' Lou stared at her. 'But
why? She doesn't do dancing. She'd be
hopeless and she'd spoil it for the rest of
us.'

'Then we'll just have to teach her,' said Emma stubbornly.

'But why?' said Lou again. 'I mean, she's not very nice and she's horrid to you. Why should you want her in it?'

Emma didn't answer. She just walked on, staring at the ground.

'What is it, Emma?' said Jem. 'Has Tracey been threatening you or something?'

'No! Nothing like that. It's just . . . she's really unhappy. I know she is. She's like I used to be . . . at the other school.'

'No one is bullying her.' Lou was puzzled.

'No, not that. But she feels left out, and sort of *unwanted* . . . I can't explain.'

'How do you know?' asked Jem. 'Did she talk to you?'

'She didn't have to,' said Emma. 'I saw her face . . . at the window. And I couldn't *bear* it.' She seemed on the point of tears and Jem put his hand on her shoulder.

'Hey! Cheer up!' he said. 'Just tell us what you want us to do, Em, and we'll get it sorted.'

They went to Miss Ashton after their next ballet class and poured out the whole story. Lou told her how Tracey had been

picking on Emma ever since she came to the school.

'But it's only because she's afraid,' insisted Emma. 'See, she's not really good at anything and she always thinks she's going to be left out.'

'Even Melanie only just puts up with her,' added Lou, 'and she's her best friend!'

Miss Ashton tried to understand. 'You think if she could be a Cat too, it would help?'

'Remember at the Summer School,' explained Emma, 'when we all did a show together, we got sort of "bonded"? I mean, we were really close friends, all of us, by the time we had finished.'

'Yes, that's true,' said Miss Ashton. 'And if Tracey was one of the Cat dancers you think it would be the same?'

'Yes,' said Emma. 'I feel sure!'

'It's worth a try,' said Jem.

'Well, I think it's crazy,' said Lou. 'She'll just fall over her feet and then get crosser than ever because she can't do it!'

'Then we'll have to *help* her,' said Emma. 'Well, *I* will anyway, even if *you* won't!'

'OK! OK!' said Lou hastily. 'Don't get mad at me, Em. You know I'll help if that's what you want.'

'I'll have a word with Miss Johnson,' said Miss Ashton soothingly. 'I'll fix it so that Tracey can be a Cat too.'

'Oh, thank you!' Emma gave her a brilliant smile. 'It *will* be all right. I just know it will!'

At break time next day, Lou and Emma were walking back from the field when

they saw Tracey and Melanie coming to
meet them. Tracey was looking very
pleased with herself and couldn't wait to
tell them her good news.

'I *am* going to be a Cat, so there!' she
said. 'It was just a mistake. They put my
name on the wrong list, see.'

'That's nice,' said Emma. 'Now we can
all be in it together.'

'I bet *you* thought I wasn't good
enough,' Tracey told her. 'Just because I
don't have lessons like you do.'

'Well, no,' said Emma. 'I think you'd
make a really good Cat.'

Tracey narrowed her eyes. 'And just
what does that mean?' she demanded.
'Are you saying I'm catty?'

Emma looked confused. 'No,' she said,
'I just meant you'd be a good . . . that you
would do it well.'

'And how would you know? You've
never seen me dancing! I'm pretty good at
the disco, as it happens!'

Lou had had enough. 'Actually,' she
said, 'it was Emma who . . .'

Emma shook her head. 'Don't, Lou!'
she said.

'Don't what?' Tracey turned to look at
Lou. 'What are you two talking about?'
she demanded suspiciously.

'You're a real pain these days, Trace,' said Melanie. 'I'm getting really fed up with you.'

Tracey looked anxious. 'Well, it's her fault,' she said, glaring at Emma. 'She's always getting at me!'

'No, she's *not*!' Lou was angry now.

'Oh, *please*!' Emma gave a cry of despair. 'Why can't we all just be friends?'

'Yes . . . well . . .' Tracey simmered down. 'Only just don't say I'm catty, all right?'

Chapter Nine

Tracey turned up to rehearsal next day in a leotard she had borrowed from Melanie. It made her look shorter and dumpier than ever and she kept pulling it down around her bottom in case her knickers were showing.

The others had been practising their cat-like dance movements for days and could all move smoothly in time together. Tracey lagged behind.

'Don't worry, Tracey,' said Miss Ashton.

'You'll soon get the hang of it.'

'I can do it,' said Tracey. She made a sudden jump, looking more like a rabbit than a cat.

'Bend your knees,' Miss Ashton told the class, 'and stre-e-etch sideways. Try to keep as low as you can.'

'I can keep *really* low,' said Tracey . . . and promptly fell over.

There was a faint ripple of laughter.

Tracey sat on the floor, her face very red.

Oh no! thought Lou. *I knew this was going to be a bad idea.*

Tracey got to her feet with a face like a thundercloud.

Lou thought fast. 'That would be a really good bit of business,' she said to Miss Ashton. 'I mean if one of the cats was a bit clumsy. It would make the audience laugh.'

76

'Are you saying I'm clumsy?' demanded
Tracey ominously.

'Well, no,' said Lou. 'But . . .'

Emma said quickly, 'It could be a
Kitten. Everyone loves kittens . . . and
they are always falling over.' She had a

sudden inspiration. 'Oh, Miss Ashton, can *I* be a Kitten? Can *I* be the one that makes them all laugh?'

'Hang about!' said Tracey indignantly. '*I'm* the one that thought of it. *I* want to be the Kitten.'

'It's a good idea,' said Miss Ashton. 'But I think two Kittens would work better than just one.'

'Whatever the Cats do,' said Jem, 'the Kittens could try to copy them and fall over.'

Everyone liked the idea, so, while the Cats practised the steps they had already worked out, Miss Ashton took Tracey and Emma to one side. She showed them how to fall and roll over deliberately while making it look like clumsiness.

When she had gone back to the rest of the class, Emma said to Tracey, 'This will be really good. I'm always scared I'll do something wrong on stage and spoil it for the others. But now, if I get it wrong, it will just look like part of the act.'

'Why would *you* get it wrong?' said Tracey. 'I mean, you do lessons.'

'Yes, I know,' said Emma. 'But I'm not nearly as good as Lou and Jem. They both want to be dancers when they grow up, but me . . . well, I just do dancing for fun.'

'Like me?' said Tracey.

'Yes,' agreed Emma. 'Only don't tell Lou I said so. She wants me to be a ballerina too.'

'I won't tell,' said Tracey. She seemed pleased that Emma had shared a secret with her.

They practised a bit more and then Emma said, 'It's great when you do the funny bits, Tracey. If you make the audience laugh, you always get the most applause at the end.'

Tracey's eyes lit up. 'You mean they all clap you and that?'

'Yes. It's really exciting . . . standing up on the stage, in front of everyone, listening to the applause . . . and knowing that the audience really liked you.'

Tracey thought about it and her face broke into a smile. 'Wow!' she said. 'It'll be magic!'

As they were walking home from school, Emma said, 'Would you like to come back to our house, Tracey, and see the kittens? We could watch them together and get ideas for our act.'

Tracey looked at her in surprise. 'Well,' she said, 'yes . . . that'd be cool.' Then she frowned. 'Only we can't come tonight, it's Mel's gym class.'

'You could come on your own,' said Emma.

'What . . . just me?' Tracey hesitated. She seemed to find it hard to believe that anyone would invite her by herself. She glanced nervously at Mel.

'Well, go on, Trace!' said Mel. 'We're not joined at the hip, you know!'

Tracey turned back to Emma. 'Well, yes . . . thanks,' she said.

They dropped Melanie off at her neat, brightly painted terraced house and climbed with Tracey up the graffiti-sprayed concrete stairs to her flat. Her mum was out.

'I'll just leave a note,' said Tracey, tearing a page out of one of her school books.

'Will your mum mind?' asked Emma. 'I mean, we could make it another night if you'd rather.'

'It's all right,' said Tracey. 'She's probably working late. If I come round your place for an hour, I'll be back first.'

'You could have tea with us,' said Emma.

'Really? Won't your mum mind?'

'No,' said Emma truthfully. 'She'll be pleased.'

Much later, after pizza and carrot cake, the three girls sat on Emma's carpet, watching the antics of Tina and Sassy. (The kittens' names had got much shorter as the days passed.)

'I had a cat once,' said Tracey. 'Well, it wasn't really mine, it was a stray. But I used to feed it bits. It really liked me . . .

used to come when I called it . . . only it
got run over . . .'

Lou and Emma didn't know what to
say. Sassy staggered across and climbed on
to Tracey's lap.

'Sassy likes you,' said Emma.

Tracey stroked the little kitten, which
began to purr.

Emma picked up Tina and put her next
to Sassy. Tracey looked up at her and
smiled.

Chapter Ten

It was the best show they had ever done because they had so many different things to do.

They found that the Cats had to sing as well as dance and the best dancers weren't always the best singers. Tracey had a strong voice, which helped to make up for Emma's rather quiet one when the Kittens sang. But that was only the beginning. They were soon painting scenery during their art lessons and helping to make costumes. The Cats wore tights with leotards or T-shirts in black or brown. Lou and Emma hunted out the ones they had worn when they were Rats in the pantomime. The brown costumes were painted with tabby stripes or tortoiseshell patches and some of the black Cats had white bibs and socks. They didn't have cat masks as Emma had hoped. Instead they wore little fur bonnets with cats' ears and Mrs Jones showed them how to do cat make-up with face paints.

'You must each learn to do your own,' she told them. 'There will be too many Cats for me to do you all on the day. I shall have enough to do sticking on your whiskers.'

They even helped to sell tickets for the concert. The Wind-up Merchant said he wouldn't miss it for the world.

'He's bought a ticket for Angela to come with him,' Lou reported to Jem.

He laughed. 'I bet she'll find she has something else to do that night!'

'Mrs Dillon bought two tickets,' said Emma.

'She's going to bring Miss Maple with her, so we'd better be good,' added Lou.

'Good?' said Jem. 'We're going to be brilliant!'

Lou sighed with pleasure. 'Oh, I do love Christmas,' she said. 'I wish we could do a show every term.'

'Perhaps you will if you go to ballet school,' said Emma.

'I don't think so,' said Jem. 'From what I hear, it's a lot of hard work!'

The costumes were finished and the dress rehearsal loomed. Tracey and Emma had their costumes padded out to make them look like roly-poly Kittens beside the lithe, thin Cats. The Kittens' part had got more and more important as everyone thought of new things they could do to make the audience laugh. It ended when the Kittens fell off the wall at the back of the stage and the Cats caught them. It took a lot of persuading before they could make Tracey do this bit: she was quite sure that the Cats would drop her. Even when she had seen Emma do it a couple of times, she still wasn't keen. But she could see that it would look good to the audience.

'Sometimes you just have to trust your friends, Tracey,' Miss Ashton told her.

'Yeah!' said Tracey darkly. 'Well, they'd just better not drop me, that's all!'

She fell off the wall at last . . . and the Cats caught her easily.

'Oh, brilliant!' she said, and climbed straight back on the wall to do it again.

The great day came and, as they all crowded into the wings, waiting to go on, Tracey panicked.

'I can't do it!' she told Emma. 'I can't go out there in front of all those people . . . I'm too scared.'

'I felt just like that last year,' said

Emma, 'when we were doing the pantomime. Only Lou explained that I wasn't really scared, only excited. She said it was the same feeling, only good not bad.'

'Well,' said Tracey, 'maybe . . .'

'Trust me,' said Emma firmly, 'and in any case, we're on now!' She grabbed Tracey by the hand and, before she could protest, dragged her on to the brightly lit stage.

It went like a dream. The audience loved the fat Kittens. They laughed in all the right places and clapped like mad when the Cats caught the Kittens at the end of the dance.

When the show was over and they took their curtain calls, the Kittens got an extra cheer. Tracey stood in the centre of the stage, holding Emma's hand, and her face shone with happiness. When the curtain fell, she hugged Emma . . . and then Mel . . . and then Lou . . . and then anyone else who came within her reach.

On Monday, when they were back in school, everyone said the Kittens had been

one of the best bits in the show. Even Mel told Tracey how funny she had been.

'And the odd thing is,' said Lou to Emma, 'that Tracey's not going around boasting about it . . . not like she used to, I mean.'

'I suppose when you really *are* good at something, you don't need to boast,' said Emma. 'I mean, *you* don't go around boasting about your dancing, do you?'

'Well . . . no,' said Lou. She gave Emma a long, straight look. 'I don't think you are going to have any more trouble with Tracey, do you?'

Emma smiled. 'No,' she said. 'I think we'll be just fine!'

Dancing Shoes

Hi!

Isn't it brilliant! Em is making friends at school and everyone, even Tracey, likes her.

I can't wait for the Christmas holidays. I hope Em's granny won't come to visit and spoil all the fun – she's really good at that!

I'm going to have to practise my ballet really hard over the holidays. I don't want to give her the chance to look down her nose at me.

Love

Lou

PS Don't forget to find out all of our latest news in *Dancing Shoes: Time to Dance.*